For Christiane

Henry Holt and Company, Inc.
Publishers since 1866
115 West 18th Street
New York, New York 10011

Henry Holt is a registered
trademark of Henry Holt and Company, Inc.
Copyright © 1993 by L'Ecole des loisirs
All rights reserved.
First published in the United States in 1994 by
Henry Holt and Company, Inc.
Published in Canada by Fitzhenry & Whiteside Ltd.,
195 Allstate Parkway, Markham, Ontario L3R 4T8.
Originally published in France in 1993
by L'Ecole des loisirs / Pastel
under the title *Flon-Flon & Musette*.

Library of Congress Cataloging-in-Publication Data
Elzbieta. [Flon-Flon & Musette. English] Jon-Jon and Annette / by Elzbieta.
Summary: Jon-Jon and Annette plan to get married when
they grow up, but war comes between them.
[1. War—Fiction. 2. Love—Fiction.] I. Title.
PZ7.E563Jo 1994 [E]—dc20   93-43771

ISBN 0-8050-3299-1
First American edition—1994
Printed in the United States of America on acid-free paper. ∞
1   3   5   7   9   10   8   6   4   2

Elzbieta

JON-JON and ANNETTE

Henry Holt and Company
New York

*E*very day,
Jon-Jon played with Annette.
Sometimes they played
at Annette's, on one side
of the brook;
sometimes they played
at Jon-Jon's, on the other.

Jon-Jon always said,
"When I am big, I will
marry you, Annette."
And Annette always said,
"When I am big,
Jon-Jon will be
my husband!"

But one night,
when Jon-Jon's father
was reading the newspaper,
he said, "Bad news!
War is coming."

The day after,
the war had come.
Papa said,
"Good-bye, my dearest wife!
Good-bye, my little Jon-Jon!
I will come back soon."
He held them close
to his heart, then
he left for the war.

The next morning,
Jon-Jon said, "I'm
going to the brook
to play with Annette."
But his mother took
him over to the window.
She showed him that
where the brook once was,
there was now a thornbush.

"That's so no one can get near us," explained Mama. "Not even Annette?" asked Jon-Jon.

"Hush!" said Mama. "You mustn't speak of Annette. It's forbidden!"
"Why?"
"Because she's on the other side of the war."

"Where is the war?"
asked Jon-Jon.
"I'm going to tell it
to tear down the thornbush!
I'm going to tell it
to get out of here!"
But his mother said
he couldn't do that.

The war was too big.
It didn't listen to anyone.
It came and went
as it pleased.
It made a terrible noise.
It ran over
everything in its way.

The war stayed such a long
time that it felt as if it
would go on forever.
But at last,
all at once, the war
couldn't be heard anymore.
Instead of noise,
there was a great silence.

That same day,
Papa returned.
He was very tired.
He said, "Finally
the war is over."

But Jon-Jon
could see that the thornbush
was still outside his window.
He said, "That's not true!
The war isn't dead!
Why didn't you
kill the war?"

His father sighed.
"War never dies,
my little Jon-Jon. It just
sleeps from time to time.
And when it sleeps, great
care must be taken not
to wake it up again."

"Was I making too much noise when I played with Annette?" asked Jon-Jon. "No," said his mother. "Children are too small to wake up the war."

Then Jon-Jon went out
to the meadow, where he
used to play with Annette
before the war.
He walked the length of
the thornbush.
All of a sudden,
he heard Annette calling him.

She had made a little hole
in the thorns,
and crossed over
to the other side
of the brook.